D0004402

Gus Makes a Gift

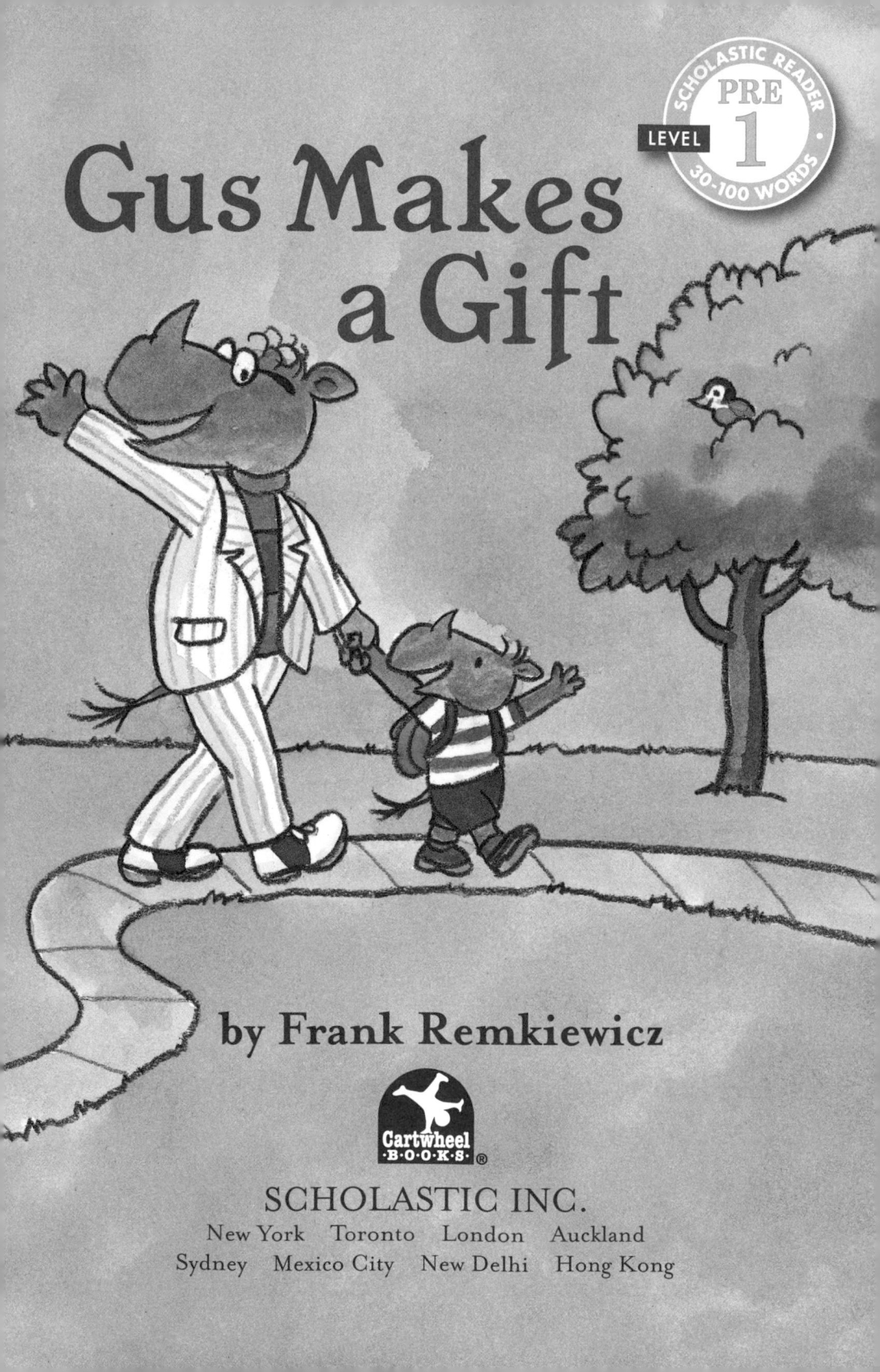

Gus Makes a Gift

by Frank Remkiewicz

Cartwheel BOOKS®

SCHOLASTIC INC.
New York Toronto London Auckland
Sydney Mexico City New Delhi Hong Kong

To Sylvia

No part of this publication may be reproduced, stored in a retrieval system, or transmitted in any form or by any means, electronic, mechanical, photocopying, recording, or otherwise, without written permission of the publisher. For information regarding permission, write to Scholastic Inc., Attention: Permissions Department, 557 Broadway, New York, NY 10012.

Copyright © 2011 by Frank Remkiewicz

All rights reserved. Published by Scholastic Inc.
SCHOLASTIC, CARTWHEEL BOOKS, and associated logos are
trademarks and/or registered trademarks of Scholastic Inc.
Lexile is a registered trademark of MetaMetrics, Inc.

Library of Congress Cataloging-in-Publication Data is available.

ISBN 978-0-545-24469-5

12 11 10 9 8 7 6 5 4 3 12 13 14 15 16/0

Printed in the U.S.A. 40
First printing, April 2011

Gus goes to school.

3 0053 01023 2315

"Bye, Dad."

Gus loves school.

It is time for art.

What will Gus make?

Gus makes a gift.

Mom will love it.

Here are some beads.

Gus likes beads.

Gus loves red beads.

Gus makes a gift.

"See my beads!" says Tess.

"See MY beads!" says Gus.

"NOW see my beads!" says Tess.

"Now see MY beads!" says Gus.

Oops!

Mom will still love it.

Gus runs home.

Mom loves her gifts.

Happy Mom's Day!